Note to parents, carers and teachers

Read it yourself is a series of modern stories, favourite characters and traditional tales written in a simple way for children who are learning to read. The books can be read independently or as part of a guided reading session.

Each book is carefully structured to include many high-frequency words vital for first reading. The sentences on each page are supported closely by pictures to help with understanding, and to offer lively details to talk about.

The books are graded into four levels that progressively introduce wider vocabulary and longer stories as a reader's ability and confidence grows.

Ideas for use

- Ask how your child would like to approach reading at this stage. Would he prefer to hear you read the story first, or would he like to read the story to you and see how he gets on?

- Help him to sound out any words he does not know.

- Developing readers can be concentrating so hard on the words that they sometimes don't fully grasp the meaning of what they're reading. Answering the puzzle questions at the end of the book will help with understanding.

For more information and advice on Read it yourself and book banding, visit **www.ladybird.com/readityourself**

Book Band 8

Level 3 is ideal for children who are developing reading confidence and stamina, and who are eager to read longer stories with a wider vocabulary.

Special features:

Detailed pictures for added interest and discussion

Wider vocabulary, reinforced through repetition

Bomb was still asleep. Matilda was cooking. The little Blues were playing a ball game but it was a game for three. No one wanted Chuck's help.

8

9

Longer sentences

Chuck went on using his rod. Three of the minion pigs crept out from behind the rocks. They snatched the old wheel, then crept away again.

Simple story structure

24

25

Educational Consultant: Geraldine Taylor
Book Banding Consultant: Kate Ruttle

A catalogue record for this book is available from the British Library

This edition published by Ladybird Books Ltd 2014
80 Strand, London, WC2R 0RL
A Penguin Company

001

Ladybird, Read It Yourself and the Ladybird Logo are registered or
unregistered trademarks of Ladybird Books Limited.

ISBN: 978-0-72328-903-6

Printed in China

Cheer Up, Chuck!

Written by Richard Dungworth
Illustrated by Jorge Santillan

Chuck was bored. He had done his morning workout three times! What could he do next? What were the other birds up to?

Bomb was still asleep. Matilda was cooking. The little Blues were playing a ball game but it was a game for three. No one wanted Chuck's help.

Red was looking after the nest.
"I'm bored, Red," said Chuck.
"Do you think the pigs will come
to snatch our eggs for King Pig?
If they do, I can help you scare
them off!"

"Shhhh!" said Red. "You'll upset the eggs! Go away and play!" So Chuck shot off.

Chuck landed on the beach. He looked about for pigs, but there was no one there. Chuck sighed. "I just want something to do!" he said.

Then Chuck saw that something had washed up on the beach. "What's that?" he said. He went to have a good look. It was a rod.

"I could catch things with this!" said Chuck. "I could catch some treasure! That would be interesting!"

The first thing Chuck caught wasn't
treasure. It was an old wheel.
"That's no use to me!" said Chuck.
He threw the wheel on to the beach
behind him.

There was something else going on behind Chuck. Corporal Pig and some of his minions were hiding in the bushes. But Chuck could not see them!

Chuck went on using his rod. Three of the minion pigs crept out from behind the bushes. They snatched the old wheel, then crept away again.

"I could use that wheel!" said Corporal Pig. He and some of his minions took it to the birds' nest.

The pigs wanted to snatch the birds'
eggs for King Pig. But first they
would have to scare off Red, Bomb,
Matilda and the Blues. The old
wheel helped them do this!

Back at the beach, Chuck had caught
something else. It wasn't treasure.
Chuck threw it behind him.
Three more minion pigs crept
out to snatch it.

The minions took Chuck's catch
to Corporal Pig.
"I could use that!" said Corporal Pig.
He used it to scare the other birds.

Chuck's next catch still wasn't treasure. It was an old trolley. "How can I use that?" sighed Chuck. He wheeled it up the beach, then went back to his rod.

The minion pigs crept out of hiding again. Chuck was looking the other way and didn't see them. The pigs wheeled the trolley away.

Corporal Pig put the trolley
to good use.
"Look out, birds!" said Red. "Pigs
on wheels, coming our way!"

At the beach, Chuck threw down his rod. "I'm still bored," he sighed, "and I haven't seen so much as one pig all morning! I'm going back to find the others!"

When Chuck got back to the nest, he was upset by what he saw. "What...? How...? When did...?" he said, looking about.

43

Chuck's morning had been boring, but the other birds had had a very interesting time!

How much do you remember about the story of Angry Birds: Cheer Up, Chuck? Answer these questions and find out!

- Who is playing a ball game at the beginning?

- Who is looking after the nest?

- What does Chuck find first on the beach?

- Can you remember two of the things Chuck catches with his rod?

- Who tries to scare the birds and take their eggs?

Look at the different story sentences and match them to the characters who said them.

"Look out, birds! Pigs on wheels, coming our way!"

"I just want something to do!"

"I could use that wheel!"

Read it yourself with Ladybird

Tick the books you've read!

For more confident readers who can read simple stories with help.

Level 3

YOU won't like this present as much as I DO! ☐

The Elves and the Shoemaker ☐

Hansel and Gretel ☐

Harry and the Bucketful of Dinosaurs ☐

Jack and the Beanstalk ☐

The Red Knight ☐

Furi on Music Island ☐

Poppet Stows Away ☐

Rapunzel ☐

Aladdin ☐

The Jungle Book ☐

Roxy and the Great Escape ☐

Angry Birds CHEERFUL CHUCK ☐

Angry Birds BOMB'S BEST BIRTHDAY ☐

Longer stories for more independent, fluent readers.

Level 4

I am Inventing an Invention ☐

Harry and the Dinosaurs United ☐

Heidi ☐

Katsuma and the Art Thief ☐

Luvli and the Glump-a-tron ☐

The Pied Piper of Hamelin ☐

Sam and the Robots ☐

Snow White and the Seven Dwarfs ☐

The Wizard of Oz ☐

The Little Mermaid ☐

Alice in Wonderland ☐

Oddie The Hero ☐

Angry Birds RED AND THE GREAT SLING-OFF ☐

Angry Birds ☐